S. RIN VOLPI

Technically Nobody

A Game Dev Novella

Contents

III Relearn

Disclaimer

This is a work of fiction. Unless otherwise indicated, all the names, characters, businesses, places, events, and incidents in this book are either the product of the author's imagination or used in a fictitious manner.

Any resemblance to actual persons, living or dead, or actual events is purely coincidental—except for the "dad," who is shamelessly based on the author's own father.

A Note From the Author

This story came about because I was tired of only reading about game development directors. Those few blessed with PR training are often depicted as the auteurs[1] of a videogame title but if you have ever watched the credits at the end of a videogame, you are aware just how massive team sizes are. Back in summer 2023, I had a spark of inspiration and thought, "Fine, I'll do it myself."

As a younger millennial, I wanted to write something that felt accessible to people in other industries where constant churn occurs. I hope that even if you do not work in games and even if you are not emotionally invested in game development that you can connect with the story.

Despite the weird jokes, this is a love letter to game development. Love hurts, no?

Thank you for bothering to pick this up.
  -Rin

---

[1]   Please read "auteur" with snark

For my dad

…and all the people championing their weird kids

Prologue

Hello, I'm an Asshole

If I do my game dev job right, nobody should know my tech is there.

If I do my job right, nobody knows who I am.

If I do my job right, the Game Director[2] won't even be entirely sure what I do.

Me?[3] I'm an individual contributor (IC). Not only am I an IC, but I'm in the Tech department. Tech Design. Tech Art. Tech Anim. We're like… the wind, oxygen, or gravity; we're needed, invisible, but there's evidence of our work if you look closely.

---

[2] You'll know the Game Director. He's the guy who can break an NDA by posting something stupid on Twitter and not get fired. Sort of like the Creative Director, but not quite—he's the guy who can lick someone's face and still get hired somewhere else. You've seen them in conference videos. He's white, with thinning or no hair, an unflattering beard, and a little potbelly. Or he's extremely buff and wears t-shirts tight enough that if he were a woman, he'd be asked to change.

[3] Also, you might wonder *where* I am. It doesn't really matter. I hail from Gamedevtopia (nobody calls it that), also known as Quebec, Canada, where the tax breaks are plenty and the buffalo are ecologically extinct.

There'll be one woman in each of those Tech- departments, probably. We Tech Designers, Artists, and Animators tend to be self-aggrandizing assholes. We're too smart for our own good, and we all equally tend to be opinionated. When I told one of my later coworkers, Camille, my theory that all Tech Designers, Artists and Animators are a little bit of an asshole, she asked if that included myself. "Absolutely," I told her. "That's why they can only tolerate one woman in the department at a time. Nobody likes too many asshole women running around together."

My trick is to make people cookies and smile when I'm being an asshole. Or send candy. Or beer.

It worked better when I was young and people thought I was naive. My very first lead told me, "Your optimism is refreshing. It's nice to have young devs around because they aren't as bitter." But I was always too anxious to be totally naive, plotting social interactions like my life depended on them. My scheming and anxious workarounds simply got better as I became more experienced in the industry.

I

Learn

Chapter 1: Stop Kissing My Cheeks

It's a special torture to be concerned with rules.

Handshakes. I learned what a good handshake was for America.[4] The right firmness. The right timing. And then, because I was cursed to be a woman, I realized different rules applied. The rules changed depending on who was shaking my hand. They might try to kiss my cheek. Or try to hug me. Or try to pretend I don't exist.

Rules I couldn't dictate.

It would have been easier to not care about social rules at all. Would have been less to learn.

Early 2013

Waiting to be introduced by my lead, I recognized the Creative Director, Michael. He'd been at JPQ, the games company I was

---

[4] I specify America because I refuse to learn or accommodate the limp headshake that people from France offer. I will not be giving dead-fish handshakes, thank you. And, of course, Canada being America's hat, we use similar handshakes.

working at, since before I was born. My heart thrummed in my throat, waiting for my manager to turn to me, waiting for the Creative Director to spot this strange little pair of lurking eyes of mine.

The introduction never came. My lead hated that guy, anyway, for reasons I could never quite pin down. I was so ready to introduce myself. Little baby tech kid that I was, I didn't know yet that men would often forget to make introductions, so I kept waiting. He glanced sideways at me a few times, and I nearly jumped into the conversation but chickened out each time.

When Michael the Creative Director left our pod,[5] my lead turned to me. "Come on, let's go to the team meeting."

"I was hoping you'd introduce me." There I went, always too blunt.

"It was a short conversation," my lead answered.

That made sense. Did that make sense?

The big meeting had lots of cool progress updates to show us. The VFX department[6] had established how they were going

---

[5] A pod was a cluster of desks grouped together, usually by subject or department. I yearned for walls, noise diffusion, and privacy even before becoming familiar with how office-plagues would rip across the white and cedar contemporary Scandinavian architecture.

[6] Not to be confused with the VFX *industry* which create virtual special effects for movies. Don't worry. We'll get to them later.

to do lava in a really inexpensive but quality way at runtime. Tech Art, Tech Anim, and Tech Design all had weirdly boring presentations in PowerPoint, even though their updates were a tour de force of achievement. For one reason or another, the tools programmers had decided to make a mock music video, so their update was by far the most entertaining. The team meeting hooted and roared with laughter as they watched.

"We're going out for drinks after," the lead character artist[7] whispered into my ear. "Want to come?"

I nodded. I'd only started at the company—in games—so recently. I wanted to make a good impression. This is what it was all about, right? Bonding and connecting and having each other's back. Exactly like when I'd finally found my people in college.

The nearest bar was a ratty old pub that hadn't been refurbished in a few decades. We weren't close enough to downtown for bars or pubs that typical business people went to, and we weren't in any of the very hip neighbourhoods where people drank after work near home. I eyed the clock. I still lived at home with my parents and would need to catch the train to the suburbs.

"You work really fast," one of the concept artists slurred at me after they'd had two beers. "I'm so glad we have the extra hands."

---

[7] Also known as modellers. They make the models. You can thank them for all the well-endowed and booty-ful characters that are commonplace in games.

I blushed and thanked him. I was proud of my work. Proud of my weird little brain for being able to do weird little things. I wasn't the smartest person to ever work in games—that would be the rendering or the animation programmers[8]—but I certainly felt like I was able to get my hands nice and digitally dirty already.

"You're right out of school, right?" he asked.

"Yeah, last year."

"How old are you?"

I cringed internally. This hadn't gone well when the other Tech guys asked me about it. One of my supposed peers had said, "I'm sixteen years older than you. I've been having sex for as long as you've been alive!" The animators had just about died when they realized the age gap, and a senior animator had asked me if I knew what dial-up internet was.

I decided on, "I was born the year *Aladdin* came out!" Most people know Disney movies, but they know them especially well in the video game industry. Games were adjacent enough to film, especially animated film.

The concept artist did the math, his eyes widening.

It was a weird sensation whenever this happened. There was a flutter of pride because I *was* proud to have made it into a

---

[8]   Don't worry about their egos getting too big; they all already know.

tech role in games at such a young age, a slither of fear that they wouldn't take me seriously, and a general wariness as I wasn't sure how they'd handle it.

This time, the concept artist simply crooned, "I remember seeing that movie in theatres."

When it was time for me to leave and catch my train, I nodded to the folks who were nestled too deep in the seating around the table to get up to say goodbye. The concept artist, though, stood and kissed me on either cheek. "A French thing!" he chimed.

The lead character artist had never kissed my cheeks before, but following the concept artist's example, he did the same when he went to say his goodbyes to me. I didn't want to resist or make it awkward; I felt lucky to be invited out, lucky to have the job, lucky to be young and successful.

Once I was settled in for the ride, listening to indie music and imagining that I was in a movie, or imagining that I was running alongside the train, I felt a little more worn down and a little more empty.

Chapter 2: Chaos and Butts

Sometimes dumb things happen, and it's nobody's fault. Sometimes it's easy to forget we're just making games. Sometimes it's easy to forget that not everyone is in the same situation as you.

Nobody wants to be the person who screams, "This train is on fire!" but hey, sometimes someone has to do it. But then, what if people don't like you? And if they don't like you, they could fire you! And blacklist you! You'll be "that difficult person," or, pray to whatever gods who'll listen, "that difficult bitch."

And then there are times you simply want to talk about butts.

2014

"It's clearly the SJW's fault!"

"They want the women to look ugly!"

I was often very confused when I read comments like these because I was fairly certain that I was one of the most social justice-obsessed women (I wouldn't call myself a warrior) around. It wasn't like I had any sway over things; JPQ was filled with men nearly twice my age. I was in my early twenties; I couldn't rent a car, much less influence a multimillion-dollar project.

I wondered: if ancient Greek gods were a thing, who in the pantheon would be responsible for dumbass comments on the internet? Or, if Christians were to be believed, "What would Jesus do?"

Shaking off the unhelpful thoughts, I went to get a coffee.

"It's GamerGate," one of the few fellow women at JPQ said to another person in the coffee nook, watching as they added sugar to their burnt-tasting coffee.[9] I eavesdropped. "They're judging us more harshly."

I couldn't place what her job was, which was silly considering there were not many women at JPQ to remember. She didn't sit with the tech people or the character folks. Writer? Designer? Something about her screamed "showy and eloquent" as far as game devs went, and I would one day compare that group of folks to scared theatre kids.

"Sorry," I blurted, "what's Gamergate?" I'd heard the word used enough times that I was scared to ask.

"How do you work in games and not know what Gamergate is?" the man asked. I knew he was a writer.

---

[9] Unlike some game companies, we never got kombucha on tap.

I stared at him. I wasn't sure what facial expression to try. I wasn't sure what to say or what socially acceptable script to follow. "Uh…"

"It's a bunch of gamers going after women in games, saying they slept their way to the top," the woman explained. "I'm sure you've heard of it."

"Oh, yeah, sorry. I guess I didn't place the name." Hadn't the internet always been terrible? Was this new?

"They've been trashing us on the forums since our latest trailer," she continued. "And they've been sending threats to a journalist who wrote a positive piece on us."

I felt a little bit numb. After thanking them, I went back to my desk and texted my boyfriend. He, too, was surprised I hadn't heard about this. Sipping my deeply acidic coffee, I watched his explanations pour in. It was endearing, but also condescending. Marc was like that. When we started dating, I liked when he explained new things to me. Since he was a little older and really into pop culture, it had been engaging and exciting. He didn't like it when I explained stuff to him, though. He sort of… ignored me. "I'm tired," he'd say.

Hunkering down to stay late that night, I put in my crunch-time-dinner order after deciding I could afford the calories. My eyes were dry from the office air, and I was fighting off the start of a sniffle.[10] Marc was meeting up with one of his university friends, and I was glad to have an excuse to miss it. I always felt stupid around them[11] because I had gone to a professional program and not a university. Not knowing the McGill and Concordia references made me feel inferior, despite the fact that I had been at a serious company like JPQ for over a year.

I thought about GamerGate.

Despite knowing the suffix "gate" was to demonstrate scandal, I felt institutionalized Catholicism sneaking its way into my mind and mused, "All are welcome past the gates of heaven, but not to work in games."

Then I cringed at modern religion in general and tried to get into a good work flow.

In the buzz of the early evening, I wrapped up a few tasks for one of the characters' butts. There'd been a lot of feedback on her butt. Too shiny, not shiny enough, funny textures, wrinkles on the clothes not changing correctly,[12] too big, too small, too perky, too stiff, too much movement, not enough movement. There was a lot of focus on her butt coming from a lot of different people.

---

[10] A thousand curses upon office planners for insisting on open-concept offices.

[11] They were also generally upper-middle-class and very, *very* boring. And that's coming from a nerd.

[12] Dynamic normal maps, please and thank you.

It was, indeed, an excellent butt. It was a butt that spoke of stairmaster journeys and a personal odyssey into posterior perfection. It was a butt that you wanted to grip, smack, lick, pat, squeeze. Your eyes could trace the curves and creases for days and days.

She had a snatched little waist and nice thighs in addition to that butt that wouldn't quit.[13]

But really, it was a bunch of adults making vectors, faces, pixels, and settings for an entirely virtual character butt. She was a goddess incarnate, endless, eternal, and probably never existing.

My pod was quiet, so I was actually able to get a lot of work done once people trickled out. When my food arrived, I kicked off a new automated process and watched it run out of the corner of my eye while I ate. I entered my food into my calorie-counting app on my phone.

My dad called. "Are you going to need a ride home?" he asked. "From the bus?"

I eyed the time. My dad went to bed pretty early, and I was nowhere near done for the day. "It's okay; I'll walk. It's not too cold."

"Want me to ask your sister?"

"If I need to, I can text her," I promised. I hated walking from

____

[13] I wouldn't let it.

the bus to my parents house after working long hours. But also, sometimes my sister made me feel incredibly guilty if I asked for a lift from the bus.

He didn't keep me on the phone. He worried about me sometimes because he'd heard me crying softly in the living room in the middle of the night from the stress. There wasn't anything to do about it. I had to do this. I had to prove myself. We lived in a safe suburb, but he also worried about me, a young woman, coming home alone at night. My family was a family of worriers. Professional worriers, almost.

"Hey, hey," someone tapped my desk. I turned in my chair, and my head was basically at the height of the cinematic animator lead's crotch. I hated that being short and sitting ergonomically meant that I routinely ended up in this position.

"Hey." I pulled out my earbuds and pushed away my crunch meal. I braced.

"So it turns out we really need the Owl-King asset before the mocap shoot," he explained. "It's nearly done, but everyone else is gone. Do you think you can get it packaged and prepared for us by tomorrow around noon?"

"Why didn't this get flagged before? I've been here doing totally different stuff." I gestured at the screen.

"Sorry, I only just, just, just realized now that it wasn't ready." He shook his head. "And my assistant producer is on vacation, so it slipped through the cracks." He hesitated. "Also, Michael[14] decided that Lady Viper needs to be totally re-worked before we finalize her."

I rolled my eyes. "Of course he did."

He grinned apologetically.

"Can I send it the day after tomorrow?"

He pursed his lips. "Maybe… I'll get back to you."

I sighed, shut down what I'd been working on, and opened up the Owl-King kit. It was mostly there, although some metadata was broken. I checked the documentation quickly and started to put it together. I stayed about an hour later than I'd originally planned; my eyes were bloodshot and tired. The crunch food wasn't sitting right with me.

Skype pinged right as I was about to run the last script to wrap up the packaging. At least it wouldn't need to be rushed tomorrow morning between meetings.

Cine Anim Lead: So it can wait until next week. The mocap guys got back to me.

Me: Jokes on you

I waited a beat while the files made it onto the network.

____

[14] Creative Director Michael

Me: I actually got it in. I'm going to head home. Let me know if there are any problems with it.

Cine Anim Lead: You're the best.

He was thirty-six, and I was twenty-two. He drove home. I rode the metro, then the bus for forty-five minutes, and then walked fifteen minutes to my parents' place. I was okay, but I was incredibly exhausted when it came time to do it all over again the following day. The whole ride back home, I wished I'd left work earlier enough that I could have at least asked my sister for a lift home from the bus.

Exhausted, I slipped into the full but sleeping house like a wraith.

Chapter 3: 5 on 10

Do you ever think about how everything is connected? I worked on a game, and a bunch of people played that game, even though they didn't know everything I did on that game. So they paid a bunch of money to a company that also paid lots of people money. We're all interwoven in our money. But then also, like, they were out there playing the game, either hating it or enjoying it, in the dark of the night or in the early morning sunbeams, between good moments and bad. Maybe they forgot their console running while they went to the bathroom, they hurried back after a phone call, or they ate dinner watching a cinematic that I poured my heart into debugging for three days.

It is so weird when you work on something and then it's out there. I wonder if people who work in manufacturing feel like this: "A car I worked on is out there." Or people who work in government: "My citizens depend on me."

And then you can think about the network of connected people and connected moments, and it goes on and on and on and on and on and on. Beautifully and horribly.

2015

"What are you passionate about in games?" a student asked me.

I loved coming back to speak at the school where I had graduated. Through my success, I was able to bring hope and fun stories and context. There was something instantly gratifying about helping out students who were in the same position I'd been in only a few years before.

They were a bit younger than I was at the time, since I had only been working for a short while. But I couldn't help but notice that as more years passed since my start date at work, the more nervous and a bit confused the students seemed to me. Had I looked like that? I must have.

"There's a sense of ownership," I told them, "more so than if you work in feature animation or VFX. There, you're only answering to a director, who is answering to a film studio."

What a stupid thing to say. Even in games, you're just answering to a *lead* who is answering to a *director* who is answering to another *director* who is answering to a *studio head* who is answering to a *VP or CEO* (who doesn't know how games are made or hasn't made games for a few decades) answering to *shareholders* answering to *conjecture*. At best, those of us in video games have no idea what we're doing. We're worse at tracking progress shot by shot and asset by asset than feature and film, so it's harder for higher-ups to self-insert into weird, low-level decisions.

If Prometheus[15] ever did exist, I think he'd resent the way we talk about corporate culture in Tech. No, really, I do.

"What's the culture like at JPQ?" another student asked me. He was wearing a dress shirt and dress shoes, standing out from the sea of faces.

Knowing that if I spoke poorly of JPQ, I could get in trouble or it could get back to them, I gave a vague and typical sort of answer. I was too nervous about my job to be honest with a classroom full of soon-to-graduate students.

Even when giving half-answers, there's a look students get when their questions are answered. That anxiety monster living in their chest is a little bit appeased, and as it relaxes, they do, too. I cannot promise them anything, but I can contextualize and demystify. After all, if I—with my frizzy hair, crooked glasses, and bad posture—can do it, they can do it, too.

"Do you still live at home?" one of the students asked the panel.

When it was my turn to respond, I admitted that I still lived with my parents. "It's only been a few years, and it's a good way to save money." The truth was that Marc didn't want to live downtown, and Marc didn't want to deal with me living downtown either. Dragging my butt to and from the studio while doing overtime was exhausting, and my disposition to motion sickness made the journey especially taxing on my body.

---

[15] Prometheus gave fire, a symbol of technology, to mortals in Greek mythology. He was condemned to an eternity of suffering for it.

However, my parents drove me nuts. They were great in a lot of ways, but sometimes it felt like I had no control and I was still tiptoeing around them, like when I'd been in school. My family loved to argue with each other, and sometimes I didn't have it in me to engage with them when I had already wanted to bash my head into a computer monitor by the end of the workday.

Marc wouldn't cave, however, so I kept putting off moving out.

"How do you deal with the poor reception of the game?"

"Honestly, I'm still figuring that out," I replied. "JPQ's *Cloud Alias 3* was a hard project to be on. It was exciting to see people excited about it on social media. It was surreal having my workout there. But… Yeah, I don't know how to deal, exactly." It had an average of "5 on 10" on most review websites. A failure.

"I really liked *Cloud Alias 3*," a girl in the back commented. My heart swelled.

"It was a mess," a boy joked back.

"Yeah, I guess, I…" the girl floundered.

"Why was it such a disaster?" the boy asked me.

I shrugged. "It's really hard working on a big game like that. It all comes together at the end, and you don't know if it'll be a mess."[16]

I wasn't even sure if I'd have a job in the next little while. *Cloud Alias 3* wouldn't be the ruin of JPQ, but it might mean big changes in the studio.

Layoffs were common in the gaming industry.

Did I have enough experience to easily get a job elsewhere?

Marc might be right. Maybe I shouldn't be thinking of moving out right now anyway.

The thoughts snaked through my worrying mind.

One of my fellow panellists took some questions about overtime. I spaced out, ignoring the way they told students they needed to crunch, to work hard, to push themselves... I'd pushed myself to the point of panic attacks for JPQ. I was worn out. I felt like sandpaper scraping on my brain when I got tired now, only able to feel rough edges.

I'd pushed and crunched on *Cloud Alias 3,* and I had nothing to show for it.

Marc, ever the unsupportive and judgmental boyfriend, didn't understand why I was spending time returning to school to speak to the students. "Only losers go back to their school

---

[16] That games successfully get made at all remains a mystery to me and everyone else working in AAA.

that much," he'd said. Maybe he was right. He couldn't be right, though. Someone had to visit schools to talk to students. Someone had to be there. Wasn't the point of success to help pull others up and along?

Someone spoke to me, and I snapped out of it.

"What has been your favourite moment in games so far?"

"That's an easy one." I beamed. "JPQ had me and a few others do a panel at Comic Con. It wasn't a huge panel by any means, but for me, it was a really big room and a really big deal." I laughed. "So I remember walking up the stairs to the stage, and then… I blacked out. Apparently, I did great." The room laughed. "And then, as I was walking to the bar with the others after it was done, it was like my brain woke back up again."

"Do you get stressed about public speaking in general?" one of the other alumni panellists asked me.

My anxiety would pop up for nearly anything, much less public speaking. However, I'd gotten very good at squashing the anxiety, pushing it to the side, and barreling through the stressors. It'd worked that far.

Smiling a little smugly, but rightful in my pride, I replied, "Compared to a Con,[17] talking with you folks is a cakewalk."

____

[17] Con as in "Conference," like Comiccon, Dragon Con, or Pax, etc.

Chapter 4: Layoffs

I'd once listened to a podcast episode about empathy in 2019 that totally rocked my world. It outlined how difficult empathy is. In the podcast episode, they mentioned that we have an easier time being empathetic if we can see and hear people; they become more real to us.

I think about that a lot when it comes to game dev leadership compared to game dev teams. How often do we really get to know people? Everyone is making impossible decisions on a razor's edge, all the while judging each other from the briefest interactions.

It's funny how hard it is to see people as people, given we're all... people.

March 2016

Following my boyfriend Marc into the pub, I was surprised that Michael[18] from *CA3*[19] was at the giant table with my boyfriend's

---

[18] The Creative Director. *Dunh dunh dunhhhh.*

[19] Shorthand for *Cloud Alias 3.*

friends.

Everyone introduced themselves, although I knew some of them already. Michael introduced himself[20] to me and Marc. He gave me a strange look, trying to place me.

"Yeah, you're my Creative Director at JPQ."

"Oh!" It clicked. He guessed my name.

I nodded. There weren't that many women to keep track of, so it wasn't too hard to remember me.

"How do you know Marc?" I asked him. My boyfriend had completely failed to mention he knew anyone else at JPQ, so I made a few quick assumptions. I tried to shake the knowledge that my lead *hated* Michael as he spoke.

"I'm married to Annabelle, and I guess she's friends with people in this group," Michael explained. "So we tagged along."

My boyfriend Marc was busy speaking with his actual friends.

"I thought you were out of town." I glanced around the table. I didn't know any of these other people. I prided myself on not being the kind of girlfriend who always needed her boyfriend around, but I hated being dropped into social situations where I barely knew people.

---

[20] Introductions in the office? No way. Introductions to a possibly random friend of a friend at a bar? Absolutely. Make it make sense.

"Just got back," Annabelle chimed. "We were out of town helping his mom, but other family members are taking over." Michael didn't add anything. I waited in case she decided to elaborate. "She had an operation."

I kept staring and put on my empathetic face. People loved to talk about themselves. Given the space, they'll say a lot. I cringed at the manipulative thought. "I hope she's alright."

"Cancer, but they caught it early," Michael the Creative Director finally provided. He barely met my eyes, while Annabelle put a hand on his shoulder comfortingly.

I didn't know what to say.

I thought that it was quite the conversation-killer.

Marc finally joined me and sat down. He didn't touch me, and he barely looked at me as he focused on Michael, immediately enamoured.

I spoke with Annabelle at length, my head buzzing a bit with the positive interaction with another woman. She was smart, funny, and interesting. She was from France, confident, and unstoppably elegant. She seemed to love Michael deeply, effortlessly. I wondered what it'd be like to be in a relationship like that.

I got into an argument with my parents that weekend because I had parked in front of my dad's car in the driveway, and I didn't get up quickly enough to shovel snow. My dad, huffing and sweaty from the job, called me a bitch in frustration. He apologized after. He meant well, but he had a short temper.

Life is kind of weird how it keeps happening and happening and happening. It refuses to stop.

When Monday rolled around, I dared to greet Michael as I passed him at JPQ. He nodded and smiled tightly.

That was weird. I thought we'd gotten along well at the pub. But he'd been weird on the weekend, and now he was being weird here. Maybe he hated me? Maybe he hated women? Maybe he hated younger people? But Annabelle and Michael seemed so great together. I replayed our interactions, trying to figure out what it was about me that set him on edge.

I remembered what I'd learnt in therapy for anxiety and tried not to think too much about it.[21] But this was different. I couldn't shake it.

There was an All-Hands meeting that was called at the last minute, and everyone filed into the large space. Nobody stood in the front of the room until the last moment.

"So much for jobs," the concept artist groaned beside me.

"What?" I blanched.

---

[21] This is not what they tell you to do in therapy. But sometimes, despite all the therapy and being good at my job, I am… not smart.

Michael took a microphone from the IT guy and proceeded to explain that we, the team that had worked so hard on JPQ's most recently shipped game, were being laid off because, after the game's failure, JPQ couldn't afford to keep us on. The other game, the other team, was already fully staffed.[22]

After gathering my things from my desk, I went out with coworkers. Michael was decidedly not invited.

We drank so much, I nearly threw up on the bus ride home. I managed to hold it until I got off the bus and threw up over the guardrail of the overpass, where there would be grass. At least I didn't puke on the sidewalk or onto the highway itself. It melted the snow that was left and made its way to the frozen soil beneath.

I was glad I wasn't currently in therapy for anxiety, so I wouldn't have to explain this to anyone.

I got home late, both too hot and too cold, stumbling to my bedroom, doing my best not to wake my parents.

---

[22] That paragraph is short and sudden. And it is. Just like layoffs.

Chapter 5: Common Mistake

It is my firm belief that it is a common mistake for women to date a mistake in their late teens or early twenties. This is obviously a generalization for which I have zero scientific backing and only anecdotal and comical evidence.

This man-mistake will define what she will and won't tolerate in future relationships. It's good to get the worst out of the way early.

2016

"It isn't working," I told him. "It hasn't been working for a long time."

I could smell his unchanged sheets and the old banana he had on his desk from where I sat in his bedroom.

"You'll be nothing without me," he said. Marc was trying to convince me not to break up with him, and this was what he went with? "You don't even have a job right now."

"I live at home." I scoffed. It was true. Fortunately, I had yet to move out of my parents' place, so I was able to take a little bit of time off after JPQ to get my demo prepared and get my feet under me. There were somehow a ton of game jobs in Montreal and Quebec City and, simultaneously, none at all that felt right for my level of expertise.

"I'm never going to be into someone as much as I'm into you."

I blinked, confused. I had to carry on conversations, and he never seemed that into me. I had to engage in *his* interests. I had to soothe his concerns while I was burning out shipping[23] the game I was on, while I was being laid off at JPQ. In groups, he barely looked at me while he seemed to gush over everyone else. Not once in our relationship had I felt supported as a person. I felt like a prop or a talking point.

"I'm sorry," I went with. It didn't really matter what he said to me, because we were over.

He shrugged dismissively as he tried to hide the hurt on his face. "You're pretty crazy." He stood and walked me out of his parents' house.

I slid into my dad's car and drove away carefully. The old car didn't have an AUX or USB input, so I relied on the FM radio's random choices to occupy myself as I drove home.

Years before, I'd been in a little bit of therapy for anxiety and

---

[23] Shipping in this case means "getting it out the door". Shipping here does not mean the same as fanfic shipping.

had been very transparent with him about it. His comment about my sanity scratched at me. He had looked for the most tender part of me and had stabbed at it in a last-ditch effort to hurt me. He'd succeeded. I didn't want to let another man cause the downfall of my mental health again.

When I got home, I cried, and my dad hugged me. My dad wasn't very good with words. My mom was out with my sister.

"How's the job hunt going?" He asked while we sat together.

"There're a few possibilities," I sniffed. "I'm worried about a lot of the options. Worried I'll somehow be both bored and stressed? Like it'll be too easy, or things that I've done over and over again, or maybe I won't be fast enough, won't be good enough."

He listened. Or maybe he was distracted, thinking about the renovations the house needed. Either way, he let me talk.

"There's a really interesting one in Quebec City," I said. "But it's scary moving away."

"You'll have a place here if it doesn't work out," he promised. He patted my shoulder, clearly keeping in mind that I often get overwhelmed by being touched too much, and he'd already hugged me when I most needed it.

Before I moved away to follow my new job, I got my first tattoo. A lot of game devs have tattoos. It was meant to be a gift to myself, some sort of recognition that I was really an adult and really free from my ex-boyfriend. Marc hated tattoos.

"But now you can only date boys who are all right with tattoos," my mom said.

"Yeah, that's fine," I laughed.

My dad shook me playfully by the shoulder, my torso bending along with the movement. "Well, at least you have a job."

II

Unlearn

Chapter 6: Anxiety

Someone once told me that game devs burn out after three years. I've never been able to find where they got this stat but game devs do apparently spend around 2 to 3 years at one company, so maybe it came from the recruitment cycle. Marginalization makes burnout even more likely.

Every year I stay in the games industry past those initial three years, I feel like I've succeeded anew.

2017

I moved to Quebec City to work at Golden Games. We called the company Golden. It was not lost on me that I was moving to a more francophone city to work at a company that had a more English-sounding name than JPQ.

Since my roommate John worked in VFX[24], I never felt like my crunch time compared at all. He would work six days a week and sometimes twelve-hour days, whereas a stressful and uncomfortable normal forty-hour workweek could make me

---

[24] Wowie, movies!

feel like ripping out my hair. No wonder so many game devs are bald.

I didn't make it a competition about who worked harder or who was more tired, but sometimes he did. He'd compare the hours we worked that day or how he often worked six or seven days a week, whereas I did my best not to work weekends unless we were very close to the ship date.

The trouble with living with John was that he was way too clean. Immaculate wasn't good enough. It got worse when he was extra tired and worn down from his crunch and work.

Blunt as ever, I asked him, "Have you considered therapy?"

"I like it clean." He ran a finger along the dining room table to check if it was clean enough. Then he crouched and scanned the floor for any reflections, dust, smudges, or droplets.

"Yeah, but this is a lot." I couldn't focus on the game I was playing on the living room TV. I felt guilty for not cleaning better, but it also never felt like enough when I did clean.

"I don't want to do therapy. I'm not crazy," he snapped.[25]

"You're pretty crazy." Marc's comment from our breakup echoed inside of me.

"Crazy." I paused the game. I clenched my body in anger.

---

[25] (Some) Men will do literally anything except go to therapy.

"Crazy? You know I've gone to therapy. It's not about being crazy; it's about taking care of yourself." I wasn't interested in mental health secrets; I was the living embodiment of millennial memes, broadcasting about going to therapy, unlike boomers.

I couldn't stop thinking about what Marc had said when I broke up with him.

Crazy. I was crazy. I'd gone to therapy. I had anxiety. I was anxious.

I refused the temptation to look up how Marc was doing. I didn't regret the breakup, but that comment stuck with me forever.

"You're pretty crazy."

You're.

Pretty.

Crazy.

We didn't live together for much longer after that. John'd apologized for the comment, but I realized that my crazy and his crazy didn't go together. We needed to live apart if we wanted to stay friends.

My solo apartment was a cute 4 ½ with really bad insulation. I don't think I have ever, to this day, paid so much for heating as I did for that place. But it was mine.

When my parents came to visit my first solo apartment, I felt incredibly awkward about the ramshackle, mismatched furniture while also being incredibly proud of the space. My dad helped me put up wall-mounted shelves, and they took me to Costco to buy a better TV. I paid for the TV myself, but at the time, I didn't have my own membership.

My dad asked if he could hug me when they left. It made me feel a little overwhelmed—my weird little brain working overtime to process how to hug correctly, be hugged correctly, the smells, the sounds, and all the other things to keep track of during a hug.[26]

The work at my new job at Golden was all right, but strange at first. The people in studio leadership seemed obsessed with hierarchy, while those on the team didn't seem to care about it at all. I had game nights at my apartment with directors in attendance, and people with twenty years of experience would pile into my apartment to play board games. Golden had less of a drinking culture than JPQ, and I enjoyed the variety in the activities I was invited to, too: paintball, movie marathons, a disappointing LAN party, and a sparse few museum trips. They still went out drinking sometimes, but it didn't have the same aggressive drunkenness that I'd become accustomed to at JPQ.

No amount of gaming parties or house decorating would get rid of the anxiety that was creeping back. Panic and fear seeped into my body, as if they were setting up shop in my bones. Sometimes, I felt like I was dying, and the anvil of anxious

---

[26] What? You're not keeping track of a million things during a hug?

expectation put a weight on my chest.

It was difficult to hate my anxiety, though.

Speaking to students in Montreal again that year, I told them, "It's like being able to see the future, but also… not. I think about stuff over and over and over. It's really useful in Tech to spot issues ahead of time."

I was a little Kassandra[27]—so good at weeding through problems. And then anxiety took hold of the reins and would ruin my delivery. It's hard to get people to believe you when you say, "This will totally break!" when they know you're anxious.

"It's just your anxiety," burned me like a sunburn whenever someone said it.

Anxiety made it difficult to get into the office. It made it difficult to get home *from* the office. Sometimes I would have a panic attack during my commute, and it felt like I couldn't feel my legs. My skin would prickle, and sweat would drip down my limbs. I felt like throwing up. I could feel everything. I could smell everything.

It was all too much. Too much. Too. Much.

---

[27] Kassandra, in Greek mythology, was a Trojan priestess. When she rejected Apollo's advances, he cursed her to see the future, but nobody would ever believe her. Sort of like epidemiologists, considering the growing anti-vax community. THANKS FOR BRINGING BACK MEASLES YOU ANTIVAX DINGUSES.

Anxiety had use if I was actually worrying about something useful, like framerate impacts when there are too many characters on screen or when the load times of cinematics are tanking because nobody set the LODs[28] up, or predicting the fall of Troy.[29]

Anxiety was *not* useful when I was so worried about the one dumb thing my dumbass manager said, days and days and days later.

Anxiety was *not* useful when I spent hours planning my outfits just to scrap them entirely and rely on jeans and a t-shirt. I had found out that some of the art team had been ranking women in the office, and every day, I was torn between presenting professionally and becoming a hag in the woods.

Despite work at Golden going well, my body was at its breaking point. I'd put off facing my anxiety for too long, and now it was a monster playing a sick, chaotic symphony with my organs. It was time for therapy again; I had to ignore what Marc and John had made me feel about being "crazy" and focus on myself.

Therapy helped.

Therapy took forever to help.

---

[28] Don't worry about it. Once you see LODs, you can't unsee them.

[29] I really missed my calling as a Greek myth by, like, a few thousand years.

Chapter 7: Managers

David. David, David, David.

2017

Okay. Listen. Truth time. Golden Games was fine. I know it had a bad reputation.[30] Really, it was fine! Well, except for my manager.

David.[31]

"That's the same lunch as yesterday." David laughed as he passed my desk on the way to his. It indeed was lunch from the same Sunday meal prep—a rationed-out, miserably small kimchi rice. I desperately counted calories to try to avoid putting on weight now that I'd moved out. So many men at work told me I would, and it was another fear added to the anxiety fire.

One day, he touched my newest work-in-progress tattoo. I

---

[30] Honestly, the games-journalism drama can miss the mark pretty hard from the real tea a lot of the time.

[31] *Daviiiiiiiiiiiiiiiiiiiiiiiiiiiiiiiiiiiiiiiiiiiiiiid.*

didn't even realize he was coming up behind me, and it made my brain leave my body.

"I can't keep doing this," I sobbed to my therapist. I explained how on edge I felt around him. I felt so judged. I tried to convince her how impossible it was to vocalize my concerns to him; he was my boss and could surely make my life more miserable. "But I can't quit. I don't feel ready to start somewhere new, somewhere else."

"We need to think about what you can control," my therapist advised me. She walked me through CBT[32] thinking traps again while I focused on all the ways David could ruin my whole career if he wanted.

In my one-on-one conversation with David later that week, he made a comment about my pay. "You're making a lot of money for your level, huh?"

What the *hell* are you supposed to say to that?

Breathing, I put on my little self-advocacy hat that my therapist had talked about. Sure, women who stand up for themselves often are less likeable, but sometimes you gotta do what you gotta do. I needed to ride that line between self-advocacy and not hurting my manager's ego.[33]

---

[32] Cognitive Behavioral Therapy. What? Am I going to teach you about games *and* about modern psychology?

[33] Nothing says woman-in-games like being in your mid-twenties and having to micro-manage your middle-aged manager's emotions.

"That comment makes me a little uncomfortable,[34]" I said.

David had lots of excuses. He apologized, but it was a shit apology.

I let it go.

The important thing, I internalized, was that I had stood up for myself.[35]

And I had to do it again. And again. And again. Each time he crossed the line, I made small, little corrections until he learned. It was like training a puppy: don't bite me, don't pee there, don't steal that, don't eat that, don't bark, and I will praise you. Thank you for treating me like a person. Thank you for treating me like my tattoo-raw skin has feelings.[36]

At least, David learned to trust me in all of this.

I was a hard worker, diligently hoping to improve the game and the lives of my coworkers. One of the more hilarious things about being incredibly anxious was that I planned very far ahead.

When concept art came up with some ridiculous asks, I had to ask David to stomp out the requests since nobody listened to

---

[34] Very uncomfortable, actually, but remember, (some) men are (sort of) babies.

[35] (Rainbows and sparkles) Therapy!

[36] And could totally get infected. I mean, what the hell? Why are you touching someone's open skin wound?

me. "Tech can't afford this new feature set," he noted. *But I had explained it to him before.*

"That specific shader tech doesn't work with the cloth tech," David explained. "We need to adjust the concept art to work with it better."[37]

It's easier when tech restrictions are coming from a manager and not an anxious, lurking, little girl. At least, it felt that way.

We found an equilibrium. I'd self-advocate delicately, I'd let him feel like he was in charge, I'd explain things to him in a fun conversational way, I'd loop him in cheerfully, I'd do a little bit of ego stroking, and then I'd go home barely intact enough to face the next day.

Self-advocacy didn't stop the panic attacks in the ladies washrooms, but thankfully, there weren't many women at the company, so I often had the space to myself.

I explained to John, my ex-roommate, about my manager David. "Do you think you maybe need to develop thicker skin?" he said once. "I mean, you don't have to care about everything," he said another time. "Sometimes he's saying stupid stuff." But of course. And my favourite: "It's just a game"—coming from the mouth of someone who worked more overtime than I did on "just movies."

---

[37] The fact that fur capes are not possible with cloth-tech has come up in multiple companies, projects, and software, and it absolutely annihilates me. Sometimes I laugh about it randomly and unprompted.

I didn't *want* to stop caring. Caring was what made me good at my job. Caring was what made me able to see something risky and flag it so we could tackle it before it got out of hand.

I thought about my experience at JPQ. Could I have cared less and gotten out a little more unscathed?

I guess my time at Golden wasn't that easy. Over time, as I mastered David's quirks, I started to pick fights with directors. I insisted on prototyping things before we committed to them, saying that they might otherwise look like garbage. I refused to make estimates on new face tech without R&D time.

As time went on, conquering my fear of David unleashed me. I was an individual contributor with a manager who might as well have been a ghost.

I was free outside those washroom stall panic attacks.

I cared about the quality, the team, the game, and my time. The directors sometimes came up with ridiculous requests, and I would tell them to their face.

"Sometimes you're so brutal," one of the Game Designers commented after a 3Cs meeting.[38]

"What're they going to do?" I joked. "Fire me?" I owned a lot of subjects. I did my best to ramp people up, but I was *fast*. David was the face, but I was the one elbow-deep in new features.

----

[38] 3Cs = Characters, Controls, and Camera.

"At least you're nice and helpful." The Game Designer was being careful and wary. "But you… could pick your words better."

When I told my dad about that line—"What are they going to do, fire me?"—he told me that I was being cocky, but he was proud of me.[39]

Despite my boldness, or perhaps due to it, I started to own more and more pieces of tech. I was included in more meetings, and people listened to me. Can you believe it? Me!? They listened! I didn't need to cower behind David's authority anymore; I could speak for myself.

The glory of owning more pieces of tech was that I could actually help people. "Hey," they'd reach out to me, "we are trying out this new feature and need some perspective on tying in with other systems." There was a thrill to being included. I always set aside time to help people.

Games were about teamwork, really. I still believe it.

How had I gotten here? From anxious and quiet and lurking… to bold and brutally outspoken?

---

[39] Dads, amirite? Simultaneously horrified and proud of their daughters.

Chapter 8: People

Don't pull the ladder up behind you.

2017

I wasn't ready for when roommate John moved away. Even though we weren't living together anymore, it hurt to know he was far away. I couldn't message him to go to a museum or a movie. And he wasn't very good at keeping up with people from back home. And I wasn't good at keeping up with people from out of town.

Golden's internal professionalism deteriorated as the game went on.

"Hey, hey," one of the Character Artists called, flagging me down as I returned to my desk from getting tea. "Do you think we can put physics on this?"

The modellers were all huddled around the desk. All men but one woman, Camille, the junior modeller.

I should have known walking into that pod would be trouble.

I'd gotten comfortable. My vigilance had faltered. I'd gotten lazy. My anxiety didn't trigger.

There was a full-frontal, naked male character on the screen.[40] They hooted and guffawed in laughter as I looked at it. Camille looked uncomfortable but had a smile stuck on her face. She was only two years younger than me, but she seemed far more fragile.

"You'll have to deal with this after us," one of the modellers laughed as he spoke to me, "but it's ok, you'll like it, because you're a girl."

Camille cringed.

I levelled a stoney gaze at him.

"Oh, come on. Don't be like that." He paled a little.

"She's too cute," one of the new modellers said. "She must think she's seen better cock than this."

I raised a single eyebrow. And stared. And waited.

I felt sick to my stomach. My anxiety tugged at my nerves, my veins, my muscles, my arteries, my lymph nodes, and my organs. I breathed slowly and deeply and didn't say anything. I willed my face not to flush and my body not to break into an angry sweat.

---

[40] Men and their love of penises, I swear to any god.

They made half excuses and strange explanations. I continued to stare.

Anything I said would make me a party-pooper or oversensitive. If I allowed it, if I condoned this behaviour, they'd think this was allowed forever.

I thought of a few women I'd known who had gotten "emotional" and how they were treated after that. People would talk behind their backs about how "difficult" they were. There had been Carla, a middle-aged Spanish programmer who had gotten into a well-deserved heated exchange, then was sidelined, and, after six months, had quit. There had been Beth, a wiry Australian concept artist who had been passed up twice for promotion, and when she had gotten angry, it had been suggested she seek opportunities elsewhere, and so she did.[41] I didn't want to have to quit. I couldn't quit right now when I was just finding my footing.

So I stared. My emotions were somewhere else. My reactions were in a secluded backup in hypothetical cloud storage. My rage was compiling on a server farm with two-factor authentication. My face and my body were flat, like a login screen without any cute background pictures.

My ever-tactless manager David[42] popped his head into the pod. Camille used the opportunity to slink away. I stared at him passively while he made light of the poorly thought-out

---

[41] She's an Art Director in a smaller studio now.

[42] Daviiiiiiiiiiiiiiiiid!

jokes that had been made at my expense.

Slowly, carefully, and with the best posture I could manage, I left the pod, went to my desk, and started to get my purse. It was only three in the afternoon, but I knew I wouldn't be productive the rest of the day.

I felt their eyes on me as I moved. None of them followed me. None of them apologized. Quiet passivity grew into tension.

I didn't rush.

I didn't say a word.

I left for the day and gave the pod a curt nod as I walked out of sight.

Let them think about what they've done.

I called my dad once I made it outside, thankful there were no smokers around the exit to witness me. I started to cry. I walked and talked and cried and cried. All the different emotions rushed out of me. He spoke with me until I got home, and then he had to go.

I tried calling John, but he was working. I left him a voice note.

I realized I had a message from Camille. She was sorry that happened, but she'd been super impressed with my composure. Apparently the others had apologized to her after I had left and said they'd realized what they'd done was out of line.

When I came in the next day, got my coffee, and went to my desk as if it were a normal day, I came across a little potted plant with all of the Character Artists' signatures in an apology. I smiled softly at them. They said sorry one last time and never made dick jokes at my or Camille's expense ever again.

Years later, I found out that when the Character Artists had been floundering, "What are we supposed to do?" Camille had suggested the potted plant and had gone with one of the senior character artists to pick it out.

The male full-frontal got cut before we shipped.

Chapter 9: Power

You may want to run full-tilt away from newly single men in power.

2018

Growing up, I always wanted a foosball table, but we never had the space. A lot of game studios have game rooms with different game tables in them. Sometimes they have pool tables. Sometimes they have ping-pong tables. And sometimes they have foosball tables.

Camille and I started to play foosball more and more at Golden. When we would go out with coworkers, we'd drift towards a pub or bar's foosball table if they had one. She was also a spectacular pool player, but I didn't like pool as much.[43]

While I had figured out how to navigate David the Manager, Camille was dealing with her own issues with the Character Art Lead. He tried to be a good manager—he really did—but Camille might as well have been an alien rather than a woman

---

[43] Bend over around a bunch of male coworkers? I think the hell not.

with the way he treated her. Why would that overly affectionate coworker make her uncomfortable? Why couldn't she speak up more? Why didn't she take bigger risks in her art?

"I have to keep explaining to him not to talk over me," Camille huffed as she bypassed my defence.

At the last moment, I blocked her shot. With a quick snap, I scored against her. "Suck it!" I shouted, my voice cutting through the bar.

Our co-workers finally found us. "We could hear you from the bar," they said, laughing.

Amidst a heated game of pool against two quick-witted QAs, Xin[44] and Brad Kim,[45] I heard someone calling my name. I didn't recognize him at first, but it was Michael, the Creative Director from JPQ. I knew from social media that he was still at JPQ, helping out on another project.

Michael kissed me on both cheeks in greeting. He smelled of oud, maybe citrus, and pretentiousness. I cringed inside a little.

I introduced him to Camille, Brad Kim, and Xin. He nodded politely and asked me if I wanted to catch up. "Want to join us for a game?" I asked. He declined, and I decided to go sit with him away from the group a little to chat. "I'll be back soon,"

---

[44] Pronounced sort of like "sin."

[45] We specified Brad Kim's last name because there were two other Brads at Golden.

I told Xin since Camille and Brad Kim were already back to playing with each other.

"You look like you're doing good." Michael touched my leg as I slid onto the bar stool. I gave him some vague platitude about Golden and shifted awkwardly. "JPQ is hanging in there. I'm actually here to meet with some consultants. Fingers crossed, we might be trying a different game for the market." He tiptoed around the secret until finally spilling it to me.

"That's exciting," I interjected as I listened. "And how's Anabelle?"

His face fell at the mention of his partner.

"She and I are separated," he sighed. He proceeded to tell me far too many intimate details. I nodded along, sipping my beer too quickly because I didn't have a chance to interject much. I made a brief and rushed statement about how Marc and I were broken up, too, and then he returned to continuing to spill his heart out.

"You live nearby?" He changed the conversation eventually.

Finishing my beer, I said, "Sort of."

"I'm staying a block away."

I stared at him. *Fuck off, fuck off, fuck off,* I thought. I had to get out of there. I knew where this was going. My bluntness, boldness, and anxiety had kept me safe from most harassment until this point; I was both able to spot problems from far away and scare them off with my unwillingness to tiptoe around topics.

Michael leaned in to whisper something in my ear. "Want to go back to my place to talk?"

My thoughts ran wild. *It's a question he's allowed to ask, and you can say no, but think about how to say no nicely because he can still make or break you if you ever want to go back to JPQ. Do you ever want to go back to JPQ? It's flattering, it's frightening, it's fucked up.* Time raced and stood still. *Was this why he was talking to me at all? What if this gets back to Marc and he's like, "Yeah, that makes sense. She was crazy."*

In my nostalgia for JPQ, Michael the Creative Director had opened me up and shirked my defences.

My eyes finally caught Camille's gaze. My eyes widened, angry, afraid, and begging. She came over and urged me to play another round of foosball with them.

"Sorry, no, I'm going to stay here," I told Michael. "Good luck with the consultants!"

I wanted to cry. Nothing had happened, right? Except I knew, from my plantar fasciitis to my chipped nail polish,[46] that I could never return to JPQ without some awkwardness.

---

[46] Or, as normal people would say, from my fingers to my toes.

I wanted to post shit all over social media.

I wanted to call my dad and John, and scream at the head of the studio at JPQ.

But instead, I played some more foosball.

Chapter 10: I'm a Star, Watch Me Burn

Don't worry. It's still only **2019**.

2019

One day when I was seeing my dad, I told him, "I'm finally making more than you." When I graduated from CEGEP,[47] I told my parents that it was possible for me to make this much money working in games and that I didn't need to go to university.

"Congratulations," he said warmly. "Don't tell anyone else in the family."

I didn't. He didn't. They still hadn't given me the "Senior" title, but that was all right. I understood that there were internal office political forces working against me.

Golden shipped the title I worked on, *Dead Set: Unkillable.* It sold fine, but it had incredibly high reviews.

---

[47] CEGEP is a post-secondary education institution—you know what? Fuck it. You can google it; I believe in you.

Despite my best efforts, I still couldn't get my dad to understand exactly what it was that I did at work. He was great about understanding the ideas behind office politics and deadlines and directors changing their minds, though. And he memorized my job title and the games I'd worked on so he could impress his friends and coworkers.

Everything was awesome.

Outside of work, we played foosball, we played board games, I biked, and I fell in love with small cafes where they started to know me by my order.

I was put on the next game prototype early. We were going to revive an old franchise, not as a sequel but as a new life in the universe. Finally, I was going to matter. I was going to be on something early. I was going to have a say. David the Manager was on a different project, and I was on a lean,[48] little pre-pro team.

I came into work every day and felt like a ragtag rogue, snaking through hypothetical tech obstacles. My coworkers and I banged out prototypes quick and early, revelling in our rakish successes, scurrying from pod to pod to grab another coworker to quickly help us hack together proto after proto.

It certainly wasn't perfect. One day after reviewing a prototype, one of the leads said to the room, "I want this to feel like when

---

[48] "Lean" is, in fact, a red flag.

I get an erection."[49] The room laughed, and a few awkward glances were made in my direction. "Sorry," he laughed.

I stared and remained silent. This had worked before. "No, please, tell me more," I accidentally rolled my eyes, walking the fine line between penis-envy and insubordination.

"Sorry." He was embarrassed under my gaze. "I want it to feel uniquely exciting."

In the quiet moments between prototypes and learning to stand up very carefully for myself, I would document. I would attend talks and conferences about diversity and inclusion. I tried to think of ways to fill my heart and soul by giving back. I'd come so far; I had finally made it.

"You are so good at documenting stuff," Camille said to me as I wrapped up a technical guideline document before we headed off to get coffee together.

"Thanks, I try."[50]

"Xin said you have the best documentation in your department."

"High praise," I mumbled. It was.

____

[49] See?! What did I say? Just like with the character-art reaction to the full-frontal. Men! And! Penises!

[50] Confluence (where the technical documentation is stored) is my bitch, and you should see my jiras.

Camille and Brad Kim had started dating, but they didn't step on each other's toes too much in the office. They gave each other space. He was trying to convince the producers that he would make a great Level Designer, but he was too excellent a QA for his own good. He'd maybe have to quit Golden in order to get the role he wanted. Xin was a QA lead now.

We were all doing awesome.

III

Relearn

Chapter 11: Brace for Impact

Pandemic.

Depression.

Climate change.

Loneliness.

Planning to quit. Golden Games had too much success. Golden was trying to be a three-project studio. Lean. Determined. Passionate. *Red flag! Run!*

But I stayed because I loved Golden Games and what it had been like on *Dead Set: Unkillable.*

My dad died.

I needed to help my mom with her computer.

My dad… died.

My mom was having a hard time setting up her yard furniture alone.

My dad died!

My siblings were arguing with my extended relatives. My mom was upset that we cancelled plans for a get-together at the last minute because of COVID.

And my dad fucking *died.*

MY DAD DIED AND I HAVE TO WORK ON A VIDEO GAME?

2020

Working in a Tech department in games is about learning and unlearning as new tech appears. One day you're rendering for PC, and the next you're dealing with VR constraints. Or you're in an out-of-the-box engine and then an in-house Engine. Maybe you're in MotionBuilder or Maya or Houdini or Nuke or Blender—although I miss 3dsMax, at least I don't need to remember how to use it anymore. Maybe you're in visual scripting; maybe you're in Python, C++, C#, or something else entirely. Maybe you're doing post-process in the Adobe Suite. Maybe you're in Jira, but maybe you're in Shotgun. Or maybe you're working from a bunch of Post-its on Miro, Teams, Slack, or Zoom? [51]

Being in Tech in games means constantly pushing for better quality results, better and faster tools, and better workflows for the team. It means looking at how the best of the best have done it and trying to imitate it. [52]

"The illiterate of the twenty-first century will not be those who cannot read and write, but those who cannot learn, unlearn, and relearn," said Alvin Toffler.

"You can't work as a Tech Artist[53], Tech Anim[54], or Tech Designer[55] if you aren't up to Alvin Toffler's standards." —Me, probably, while shouting into various social media voids and trying to cope with the ever-mounting stress of working from home during a pandemic after my dad died.

Grief broke my memory.

I bought rice three times in a row at the grocery store because I couldn't remember what I had at home. I kept buying chamomile tea until my entire tea shelf was chamomile tea. I was like an Alzheimer's educational commercial from the

---

[51] If you didn't get it, that's okay. That's the point.

[52] and and and my dad died.

[53] Tech department shaders, tools pertaining, but not limited, to environment art, etc.

[54] Tech department animation, tools and integration pertaining but not limited to animation, etc.

[55] Tech department largely helping with gameplay, design logic, and workflows.

'90s, but instead, I was a woman in her late twenties, doing her absolute best.

Grief shattered my mind and dropped me into a hazy fog.

I was unmotivated. I was disoriented. I was tired. I was spaced out. I used to be so wired and on the ball. I used to be two steps ahead. I used to have the best work documentation. I used to care. I used to care so much if we were allowing too-risky features into the game. Now I could barely keep up with a conversation about anything new.[56]

Grief stripped me of my hobbies. The pandemic stole many of them, and grief made the rest a chore.

My weird little brain, which used to be able to do weird little connections, couldn't do it anymore. I panicked; what if I couldn't do my job at all anymore?

What if I was useless?

What was I supposed to do if I couldn't make video games? I didn't have any marketable skills other than this, certainly not six-figure-salary skills. I had lived in a gilded cage for years, and now I was fighting and clinging to it desperately, unsure if I could keep up.

The tangle of nodes in the engine graph looked like medical

---

[56] My dad died, and I'm making a video game, and I'm trying to seem fine and normal by making a game fine and normal and fine and normal.

tubes, which were hugely ineffective when executed too late. I couldn't follow them.

I felt like I couldn't read.[57] I reread the same word over and over and over.

I felt like I couldn't learn.[58] I metaphorically clutched documentation because I couldn't internalize the new plugins, workflows, and tech. I apologized when people needed to remind me of where buttons were and what different settings meant.

Learn.

Unlearn.

Relearn.

My whole life, my whole career, I did my best to learn the rules: from introducing myself, handshakes, to how to present myself to others. I learned and followed the pandemic rules. I followed them and followed them and followed them and everyone else skirted them. My dad learned and followed the rules for himself. He worked and had kids, and he was a mostly good man, and he died before he could retire.

Grief is hard enough when there isn't a pandemic to force us to

---

[57] Between each word read, I think about my dad lying in the hospital bed, a little vacant and confused.

[58] Between between between just grief and processing and why why why.

hold the saddest, smallest funeral ever for someone who was really important and deserved more.

Learn grief. I mean, cloth sim.

Unlearn grief. I mean, an old engine.

Relearn grief.

It never stops. I am Sisyphus,[59] and my boulder is new games and new technology. I am Sisyphus, and I can't even see the boulder that I'm pushing up a hill anymore. It never stops. I am Sisyphus, and I am desperately trying to prove that I can roll boulders up a hill very well, very politely, very professionally, very quickly, and very elegantly.

I am Sisyphus, and I am trapped.

Dad, I want to tell you about this shitty thing that happened at work today, but I can't even remember what it is anymore. The rendering programmer had to explain it to me twice, and I had to rewatch a recording of the meeting before I finally got it. I'm worried that they'll realize I'm struggling and fire me.

What am I going to do if I can't do this?

For years, game devs had wanted to eat me up and spit me

---

[59] A Greek myth about a king who was cursed to roll a huge boulder up a hill for tricking others. Sisyphus killed people, though, so I am pretty sure he deserved his boulder-rolling more than I. If I have angered the Greek gods to curse me in such a way, they sure haven't explained why.

out, but I fought. I stuck around through being casually hit on, through layoffs, and through stupid dick jokes. I fought and I fought, and I stayed and I stayed. I stayed despite Michael and John and David and Marc. I stayed with my Camille, my Xin, and my Brad Kim. I wound my whole life around this job.

Dad, what if I can't be a game dev without you?

Chapter 12: Values

Content Warning : This chapter deals with some indirect suicidal idealization.

Wordsmithing will be the death of me.[60]

Employee Resource Groups (ERGs), in many forms, are there to make advocates waste their energy and feel like their company has their back rather than making effective change.

Never ever join an internal group designed to come up with any mission statements or pillars. Do not participate in things that do not have transparent benefits for those demographics.

You are right to laugh, cackle, guffaw, giggle, sniffer, chuckle, chortle, howl, and roll on the floor laughing if you are ever presented with lukewarm company-speak that boils down to "power, determination, and having a very lean team," since that is not only a red flag, but a very lazy one, too.

I kept my physical mask while I did my best to cast aside my

---

[60] I say, while writing all this down.

metaphorical one. When I tried to mask again, sometimes it hurt. It hurt not to mask, and it hurt to mask. The pandemic gave me an opportunity to play with that.

Unfortunately, that makes it very difficult to masquerade in front of studio-level wordsmiths.

2021

Golden Games started to have meetings with individual contributors—people like me—and leadership. They wanted to understand how to make the company culture better. They wanted to understand how to be better. They wanted to touch base and make sure we were doing all right. They randomized who would be in which meetings.

Xin had their meeting the week before I did. "It was pretty useless," they explained. They didn't commit anything like that to writing and only told me while we played some co-op multiplayer games online together.

The Golden Assistant Studio Head, Gale, kicked off our lunch meeting with a chipper explanation that they were trying to improve the studio. The remote meeting involved conversation, her note-taking, and a very brief virtual post-it board.

I ended up on the call with one of the Character Artists and several programmers.

When we tried to have a conversation and give feedback, though, Gale would cut us off. She always had something to say.

"Other studios are facing the same struggles as us."

"Unprecedented times."

"We have a slow return-to-office plan, but we aren't planning on forcing anyone back into the studio if they don't want to return. But you should come!"

Gale was the epitome of corporate culture's "good vibes only."

I missed my foosball table with Xin, Camille, and Brad Kim.

When the only other female individual contributor in the call asked, "Why hasn't Golden taken a stance against TERFs? Why has Golden struggled so much with diversity and inclusion? We keep losing women," I was not entirely surprised that Gale had a very corporate response ready to go.

I wrote to Camille in a separate chat, "I understand that Gale can't exactly say whatever she wants because she has to represent Golden, but this bullshit is exhausting."

"And you?" Gale called on me. "Did you have anything you wanted to add?"

I thought about a myriad of my past game dev experiences. I thought about ERGs[61] and my time at JPQ. I thought about COVID and my dad and climate change and the Roman

---

[61] ERGs are Employee Resource Groups, which are notoriously ineffective initiatives. I said what I said.

Empire[62] and Patroclus[63] and roosters and the Huns[64]. I thought about the Silent Revolution and the injustices that went into building the Canadian railway and the fact that many indigenous communities still didn't have water, and the fact that we were all on a rock hurtling through space. I thought about how it was really weird that the sun and moon appear to be the same size from our point of view.

I thought about nothing.

I thought about everything.

Gale didn't care.

I didn't have the energy to explain any of this to her so that Golden could pretend they'd done something. My weird little brain was strangling itself on node graphs. I couldn't give Gale any of my energy. All my mental energy was used to scrape by and barely manage to do my job.

So I went with, "I'm too depressed to mince words, so I don't see the point in saying anything in this meeting."

"I'm sorry to hear that," she said. "Don't hesitate to reach out if you ever want to talk one-on-one."

---

[62] I would learn in 2023-2024 that a lot of people are idly thinking about the Roman Empire, so I'm not alone in this.

[63] Achilles' almost-certainly-queer-lover from the Iliad.

[64] If you're going to think about empires, you also want to think about the Huns.

"Thanks."

Therapy wasn't really helping anymore.

David the Manager reached out to me after the meeting, doing his absolute best to be helpful, but not really having anything useful to say. He had come a long way as a manager, but my despair and disillusionment were beyond his pay grade— pushing on existential and spiritual. I wished, not for the first time, that I believed in literally any god or gods.

Nothing mattered.[65] The game didn't matter.[66] The studio didn't matter.[67]

My dad was dead, and maybe he didn't matter.

I didn't matter.

Even after that, I tried to tough it out. I wanted to stay. I had enjoyed working with Xin, Camille, and Brad Kim. I had found equilibrium with David. I knew the tools, the tech, and the people. I was too numb to enjoy any of those things, but at least they didn't hurt. Somewhere along the way, I had forgotten how to feel good. Somewhere along the way, making games felt like absolutely nothing.

---

[65] My dad was dead, and the pandemic wouldn't stop.

[66] My dad was dead, and the pandemic wouldn't stop.

[67] I could just work and work and then die before retirement. Or when society collapses. Or when climate change comes for us all.

Leaving for burnout was an option, but being trapped at home in lockdown wouldn't do much good. So I pushed like I had in school. I pushed like I had pushed for *Cloud Alias 3*, years earlier. I pushed like I had when my dad was dying. I pushed forward because stopping almost certainly meant I would never work in games again and never make this sort of money again. Pushing because you *have* to does not help with burnout.

It all came to a head one day when I was in a review meeting, exhausted from my brain fog, worn out from my memory loss, and stretched thin by the expectations of the "lean staffed" project. There was no forced overtime, but I was still pushing extremely hard every day.

"And zen ze tubing," Richard segued.[68] He was the somewhat new Creative Director at Golden Games. "It looks…" He paused. "Cheap."

Tubing. My tubing. The tubing I had banged out in record time was being called cheap. The tubing I had been sort of proud of to have managed not only in these "unprecedented times" but with my stupid bad brain and my under-supported role. My tubing that I couldn't feel real joy over but had managed a little shred of happiness and pride anyways. My tubing that I'd built with rickety tech, like a scaffold made of sheer force of will.

My. Fucking. Tubing.

---

[68] Please read in a heavy accent as seen in the internet masterpiece "End of ze world" from the early 2000s.

Rage cut through my bland, depressed reverie with one re-sounding and clear sentiment in my heart that I could still not be bothered to voice aloud: *"Fuck this."*

I left the meeting.

I opened LinkedIn.

Almost immediately, my various social media algorithms[69] knew I was looking for work.

---

69 Including TikTok, which, like, how?!

Chapter 13: The Apocalypse Will Be Broadcast Live

Content Warning : This chapter deals with some indirect suicidal idealization.

"**Peter** and the <u>rooster call</u>" is written in my notes, and I don't know what this even means.[70] I'm a ^{mess}.

```
I'm figuring out the memory loss but getting more
depressed.
```

I'm job hunting by morals or values rather than by game, but maybe that's not even enough. Golden is too thin, too starved, too nothing, too much.

Politics, climate change. Oh my god, what am I even doing? Why am I working in games when it's the APOCALYPSE outside?

---

[70] I'm kidding, it'll come back around, I did edit this.

I wasn't suicidal, but I wasn't especially interested in being alive.

```
The only way to console myself was that we were tiny,
meaningless nothings on a rock hurtling through
space. So why bother trying? Why bother doing
anything?
```

I grit my teeth against layoffs—my GOD. LAYOFFS? AFTER THE LAST TWO YEARS?—and I proudly worry about protests or strikes or collaborations, or whatever else I'm absorbing through osmosis on social media.

2022

I moved back to Montreal and started to work at Plus1Games, often shortened to P1G. Game studio names really are the stupidest things once you become disillusioned with them. You could probably pick nearly any noun or phrase and use it as a game studio name. Some people think up band names, but I think up studio names.

- Roman Achilles Games
- Drop Dead Gorgeous Games[71]
- Ambassador 514[72]

---

[71] This would be great for a visual novel company, please and thank you.

[72] 514 is the area code for Montreal phone numbers.

- Interrobang Not Included (INI)
- *"Stop saying you advocate for diversity and inclusion when you are a new company made entirely of white men and one white female HR lady"* Games

See? I'm amazing at this.

Fortunately, there's no shortage of halfway acceptable game-studio name ideas. Exactly like there's no shortage of white middle-aged directors branching off to make their own game studio with the self-assured certainty that *they* will be different.

Michael the Creative Director[73] joined the flocks of men who started their own game studio, thinking they'd be better and they'd be different. He hired all of his friends, and their social media posts are endearing and perfectly accessible. I screamed about it to Camille while we virtually body-doubled, and she consoled me as best she could.

It made me sad to leave Quebec City to move closer to home. I was sad to leave behind Camille, Xin, and Brad Kim. They weren't far away, and everything was still being done over Zoom. We played games. Xin came out as nonbinary. Camille and Brad Kim got engaged. Ex-roomate John moved back in with his parents.

---

[73] You remember Michael, the guy who hit on me shortly after I'd been laid off at a company he still worked for? Hit on me when I was really young, the MOMENT he and his wife separated?

The thing about P1G was that they didn't pay as much, but they had an excellent work-life balance. They hired me as a Senior, finally.[74] My ex-roommate John made a shitty comment that I was "finally" a senior. Sometimes he's a jerk like that, but at least he still messages me regularly. I'm sure I'm an asshole[75] to him, too, sometimes. We're all trying our best.

Why work in games?

Why work at all?

Why be alive?

Why roll the boulder up a hill? Why let the birds peck out someone's liver so I can make stupid games so some shareholders can make money? I am Sisyphus, I am Cassandra, I am not worthy of Prometheus' gift, and neither are *you*, and after all this time, the technological fire is burning me out.

Why? Why, why, why, why, why?

The real thing that made me leave Golden, though, was when they refused to acknowledge the Very Shitty Things that were happening to the Black community, trans folks, and sexual reproductive rights in the United States. For years, I'd joked, "What are they going to do, fire me?" But in the end, I couldn't tolerate them anymore, so I joked that I fired myself before

---

[74] Despite incessant positive feedback, all my male peers from school had been seniors or leads years before. So weird. I wonder why?

[75] I am, in fact, always a bit of an asshole. We've established this.

they had a chance to do it. A lot of people quit because of the working conditions, but, really, I quit because Golden's toxic positivity made me resent the wet noodles masquerading as leadership. It seemed I would suffer fools, but I would not suffer cowards.

"Have you considered a job outside of games?" my therapist asked me. "Or working for a much smaller company, maybe?"

"There's no way for me to make this much money in any other industry."

I was good at what I did, but I wasn't a programmer or software engineer that could work in non-game tech. I was good at navigating *this* industry, but I didn't think other industries would tolerate me, much less pay me well. "I can't afford my condo if I don't make this much money—and it's only a *loft*." I had no children, a secondhand car with no payments, but being a single-income-household in a time of great inflation made me feel on edge.

"I have to work in games," I told her, "but I need to find a way to be okay again." This was the boulder I'd chosen, but how I rolled it up the hill needed to be in my control.

"Then we need to talk about ways for you to work in games and take care of yourself," my therapist told me.

So I stopped asking myself, "*Why* make games?" and started to try to ask myself, "How could I make games and still keep going?" If rolling the metaphorical boulder up a hill was going to happen no matter what, how could I do it in a way that I could recover, survive, and still feel whole?

When I die, and if Saint Peter exists,[76] I will be confident in my decisions when I stand in front of the doors of Christian heaven. There are some things we can't avoid in life, since capitalism and consumerism crush us, but I will do my best. I will walk up to the pearly gates, and he will smile at me. If he doesn't, well, I am confident in my decision-making, and Saint Peter can suck it.

When I die, I hope I hold my tongue if my heart is weighed against the feather of Maat.[77] If Maat, personification of justice, ever wants a snarky mortal substitute, I am of course bound to be available shortly.

The only way for me to rediscover joy after my great personal apocalypse was to hold my values above all else. I will, because I have to, wear my heart on my sleeve for daws to peck at.[78] I will screw my courage to the sticking place.[79]

Conviction is what I have to have learned, or else I might not have learned anything at all.

---

[76] Which I don't believe, but that's a moot point.

[77] Ancient Egyptians believed that if a person led a good life and their heart was of equal weight to a feather's, they were worthy of living in paradise forever. Which really just seems like a physically unreasonable standard.

[78] Couldn't do this without a Shakespeare reference.

[79] Ok, one more Shakespeare reference. Or a Disney's Beauty and the Beast reference.

Chapter 14: It Sucks, and then One Day You're Okay

Losing my memory and encountering debilitating brain fog changed me. Everyone else decided to go back to normal, but I knew I couldn't. I clutched my returning functions and faculties. I will not let the rooster mock me; Saint Peter can suck it.

2023 - Ten Years in Games

I lost touch with Xin when they moved to Europe. They don't really post on social media anymore, ever since our feeds on Twitter became even more of a cesspit. Camille and Brad Kim are engaged, which is cool, but now that things are "back to normal," they're never available to play games online. "We have an open-door hangout policy!" But when in the hell am I ever in Quebec City?

I learn.

Catching up with my ex-roommate John, I told him I was finally on an antidepressant for depression and anxiety. "I assumed you already were," he mentioned. "I'm glad you're getting the help you need. Is it helping?" He's grown a lot since he made me feel crazy for getting help.

"Yeah, I'm able to enjoy way more hobbies." I listed them.

He tells me about his overtime. He's moving back to the city. I tell him how, years ago, the comment he made about therapy being for crazy people, had cut so deeply, and he apologizes. We'll hang out more when he's here.

I unlearn.

I engage in conferences that are still COVID-safe. I volunteer to help with political campaigns, even though I'm always the only person masking. I make new friends—a smooth-talking, rogue anglophone named Lilly, a soft-spoken Muhamad, and a very spicy nonbinary Australian named Ollie. Making friends as an adult is difficult, but I keep to my personal emotional razor about aligned morals and values.

I don't worry if men don't introduce me in meetings anymore. I don't really care about them if they can't be bothered to make those introductions. They're probably boring anyway.

Over the years, I've internalized that I can't tell my dad about what's going on in my life anymore. I can't rely on him to help me pick out TVs or do home repairs.

I relearn.

Am I ever going to feel like I've given enough? Connected

enough?

P1G isn't a perfect game studio, but at least I can focus on my workload. Sometimes I miss the feeling of being a formidable tech force at Golden, touching on as many topics and features as possible. But doing a deep dive at P1G isn't so bad.

My memory is coming back. My ability to focus is rekindled by clearly defined tasks and a reasonable scope.

I miss my dad. That never goes away.

There's some really cool tech being developed for this project, and I'm starting to believe the various programmers I work with are starting to enjoy collaborating with me. More and more people at P1G are figuring out who I am, and I'm once again owning some features and becoming a point of contact.

When I close off bugs, I think to myself, "Thanks, weird little brain."

Chapter 15: Ship It

$$2000 + X + Y + Z^{80}$$

If I do my job right, you won't even know I was there. You'll know the CEO. You'll know the Directors. But you won't know me.

My digital fingerprints in the game will be invisible. I wonder if I could try to be like that in life. Just kidding. That would be too simple. Imagine if that could work: I am the wind, I am gravity, and then one day I'm gone with no significant climate impact? The dream.

In reality, I'm the weirdo who is responsible for figuring out dynamic snake movements or systemic creepy tentacles. I'm the weirdo who specializes in splines for a project so we can get performant, adjustable tentacles, and then on another project, I hyper-focus on procedural gore. I am the asset-fairy; you put a

---

[80] Get it? Because we use X, Y, and Z axes in 3D? So glad I explained that joke.

jira[81] under your pillow at night, and in the morning, you find simulation settings and pipelines.

There's no one truth. I get lost in my self-reflection sometimes. I'm a bunch of bacteria in my gut, wrapping around other organs and hormones and skin and muscles and neurotransmitters, and maybe the wrong amount of vitamins.[82] I'm a timer, tick-tick-ticking away out of sync with the world, but somehow in sync with my computers. It would be easier if I could swap out my brain's graphics card every few generations.

What's one woman's perspective? What's one person's perspective? What a massive undertaking it is to make games! I can't believe it ever works out. How could I be such an asshole to think I could contain it all in a novella, not even a novel? Not even a series? Not even a lifetime?

Lay back and watch the moving parts. You don't need to touch all of them or even represent all of them. You only need to care a little bit. And keep going. Don't deny your values as the rooster crows, because most people are too much of a coward to turn you into the Romans[83] anyway.

Struggle. Fail. Ship.

---

[81] Jira is a task-tracking software often used to keep projects organized. My attitude towards Jira is quite lawful-evil; I refuse to do a lick of work if I don't have a jira for it.

[82] Being an adult is exhausting.

[83] This is a reference to Peter denying Jesus after Jesus was taken away. That would, of course, be before Peter got to park it in front of the possible pearly gates and judge everyone *else*.

It will be absolute hell, but one day you will see the stars again.[84]

Rest. Learn. Unlearn. Relearn. Rest. Learn.

Keep going.

Keep going, Sisyphus; I believe in you.

Ship it.

---

[84] Shoutout to the last line of Dante's Inferno.

Final Authors Note:

Firstly, let me thank my friends who put up with reading all my weird trash over the years ever since I started writing again. Thank you especially to the people–Alicia, Sarah, and the writing group at Suspicious Fish–who tolerated the very early work-in-progress. Thank you to Catherine, Ian, Louisa, Greg, and Dana for reading the versions that finally started to seem real. Thank you to the friends who answered the polls on what to title the novella and the people who pointed out my first pass of titles all sucked. This really wouldn't be what it is without my copy editor[85] and cover artist. Despite all the education I've received, commas and colour theory make me glad that I can rely on masterful people like you. A special shoutout to my therapist; I can't wait to talk about any bad internet reviews with you.

My dad was a huge support of my professional life and I didn't fully appreciate it until he passed away. Despite the fact that I hadn't even returned to hobby writing until after my dad died, I have to thank him for the role he played in making me into the

---

[85] I wrote this Final Authors Note after my copy editor had already done a pass so if you see mistakes, know that it is because I didn't strictly expect anyone to read it.

kind of hard-headed and loveable goofball who has way more follow-through than necessary in a human body. Similarly, I wouldn't be good at my job if not for my dad because he set me up with my first 3 ½ floppy, gave me anxiety to overthink things, and the confidence to fix them. Thanks, babo.

You will see a lot of me in this book. They say write what you know and I sure did. However, I promise, the main character is not me. Among other things, I'm way gayer and way less composed. Plus, the main character probably even knows how to use commas properly.

Naming characters was both easy and difficult. I knew I needed to have a "Michael" and a "David" in name to represent the impressive amount of Michaels and Davids (in spirit if not in name) I've worked alongside. Feeling very clever, I denied the narrator a name in her own story to keep that individual-contributor anonymity.

Finally, writing the ending was exceptionally difficult because it never really ends. You just keep making games and trying to heal the broken parts as you go. There is no happily ever after in game dev. Just another shipped title.

I guess I better ship this, too.

-Rin

Meet Your Creators

<u>Cover Art by Angela Chiarelli</u>

Angela is a Montreal-based Character Designer and Animator with a passion for storytelling. She studied at Dawson College and completed two technical degrees in both Professional Illustration and 3D Animation & CGI. She's been working as a professional freelance artist since graduating as she continues to build up her portfolio with aspirations to work in the film and/or video game industry.

You can check out her portfolio at <u>https://angelachiarelli.portfolio.site</u>

<u>About the Author</u>

S. Rin Volpi was born and raised in Montreal, Quebec. After graduating from Dawson College's 3d Animation and CGI program in 2013, she began working in games in 2014. At the time of publishing this novella, they have shipped five AAA titles as a Technical Animator. Despite still not having a good grasp of how to use a comma, he has taught intermittently at Dawson's 3D Animation and CGI program since 2020.